THE DARKEST HOUR

VigrasH
THE CLAWED
EAGLE

With special thanks to Allan Frewin Jones

www.beastquest.co.uk

ORCHARD BOOKS
338 Euston Road, London NW1 3BH
Orchard Books Australia
Level 17/207 Kent St, Sydney, NSW 2000

A Paperback Original
First published in Great Britain in 2013

Beast Quest is a registered trademark of Beast Quest Limited
Series created by Beast Quest Limited, London

Text © Beast Quest Limited 2013
Cover and inside illustrations by Steve Sims © Orchard Books 2013

A CIP catalogue record for this book is available from
the British Library.

ISBN 978 1 40832 399 1

5 7 9 10 8 6 4

Printed and bound by CPI Group (UK) Ltd, Croydon, CR0 4YY

The paper and board used in this paperback are natural recyclable
products made from wood grown in sustainable forests. The
manufacturing processes conform to the environmental regulations of
the country of origin.

Orchard Books is a division of Hachette Children's Books,
an Hachette UK company

www.hachette.co.uk

VIGRASH
THE CLAWED
EAGLE

BY ADAM BLADE

ORCHARD

Dear Reader,

My hand shakes as I write. You find us in our hour of greatest peril.

My master Aduro has been snatched away. The kingdom is on its knees. Not one, but two enemies circle our shores – Kensa, the banished witch, has returned from Henkrall. With her stalks Sanpao, the Pirate King. Strange magic is afoot, stirring not just in Avantia but all the kingdoms, and I sense new Beasts lurking.

Only Tom and Elenna stand in the way of certain destruction. Can they withstand the awful test that will surely come? This time, courage alone may have to be enough.

Yours, in direst straits,

Daltec the apprentice

PROLOGUE

"Stop squirming now, my lucky lovelies," said Kurt as he staggered along under the weight of a sack full of rats. "Eat the food I've put in there for you. You'll soon be let loose."

These were busy times for rat-catchers, and Kurt was one of the best. He never used poisons to deal with the swamp-rats swarming through the streets of Meaton. He used wicker traps that caught the creatures without harming them.

Every morning, he would leave the town with a wriggling sack full of rodents, and walk to the desolate Marshlands, where he would set them free.

He plodded along the track, his ears full of squealing. "You probably don't know it, my pretties, but strange things are happening in Kayonia," he muttered. "It used to take me all morning to walk from Meaton to the marshes, but now it takes no time at all."

The marsh seemed to be advancing on the city – as though the whole kingdom was shrinking.

Kurt passed the twisted tree that marked the beginning of the marsh. Rustling grass rose up all around him and the ground became boggy. The smell of rot and decay filled his nostrils, causing him to draw his scarf up over his nose and mouth. These marshes were the spawning ground for the rats and it was from here that they would stream into the city, terrifying everyone.

"And what's the harm if a few of the rats I release into the marsh find their way back to the city?" he muttered gleefully. "I'll just catch 'em all over again, and get twice the bounty!"

He looked over his shoulder. A thin greenish mist always hung over the marsh, but he could still make out the towers and rooftops of Meaton in the distance.

"This will do," he said, gently setting down the sack and untying it. "Off you go, my sweeties."

Brown rats and black rats and

cream-coloured rats jostled and clambered over one another, squeaking merrily as they surged out of the sack and into the marsh.

Then, very suddenly, the rats all stopped, their beady eyes gleaming, their whiskers quivering. A moment later they all took off in the same direction, swarming in a pack, squeaking in fear.

The hair on the back of Kurt's neck bristled. The mist swirled around him. He could sense something approaching – something horrible.

He picked up his sack and trudged off to high ground, hoping for a clearer view. "Is anyone there?" he called, his voice quavering a little.

A dark tide of rats ran past, squealing in terror, their feet pattering, their long tails rustling,

bodies bumping as they fled some
unseen menace.

Kurt tripped over the seething mass
of rats and crashed to the ground.
As he lay gasping, he saw something
looming above him in the mist.

A creature hovered over the marsh
on gigantic black wings, like some
kind of monstrous bird. Trembling
with fear, Kurt stared up into its deep
black eyes, then at the cruel, curved
yellow beak.

But it wasn't an ordinary bird – it
was something far more dreadful.
Its four-legged body and tawny fur
was more like a cat's – and its claws
looked deadly enough to tear Kurt
to shreds.

This is a Beast, Kurt thought as he
began to crawl away as fast as he
could, knowing now what it felt like

to scurry for his life like a rat.
But when he heard the sharp

cry from the creature, and felt the draught of its wings, he knew he would never be able to crawl fast enough…

CHAPTER ONE

FLIGHT INTO PERIL

"Farewell, and may good luck go with you on your next Quest!" The words of Daltec, Aduro's apprentice rang in Tom's ears as he sat astride his horse, Storm. Elenna sat behind him and Silver the wolf stood close by.

Daltec clicked his fingers.

At that moment everything changed. Tom lurched in the saddle, staring around as fields, hills, rivers

and mountains flashed by in a blur.
The landscape of Gwildor was flying
magically past them.

Tom felt a mixture of exhilaration
and alarm as a dense forest fled away
on either side. "This is a strange way
to travel," he said as they whipped
through the branches.

There was a grin on Elenna's face. "Daltec has learned a lot from his master," she said. "Think how long it would take us to come so far on foot. We're travelling like lightning."

They shot out of the forest and sped at a dizzying speed through rugged foothills and over bleak mountain passes. Moving faster than the swiftest arrow, they were whisked down to a rugged shoreline and out over the sea.

But Tom's mood had darkened at Elenna's mention of lightning. It was lightning that had been the cause of their problems. Their wizard friend Aduro had helped them use the Lightning Path to travel between kingdoms and hunt a powerful, dangerous witch named Kensa. She was using Beasts to threaten the peaceful land of Henkrall.

Tom had succeeded in destroying Kensa's Beasts, but the witch did not wait long to fight back. She had fled to Avantia, and broken Sanpao the Pirate King out of his prison. Together they had escaped in Sanpao's flying ship.

As if that wasn't enough trouble, Tom learned that Kensa's magical method of travel had accidentally released six monstrous Beasts from their Lightning Prisons. They were Beasts of old, whose evil rage was upsetting the natural balance of the worlds, pushing Avantia, Gwildor and Kayonia closer together.

Travel by the Lightning Path was forbidden, and Aduro had been put on trial by the Circle of Wizards and stripped of his powers. He now lay in a prison cell, and the Judge would only release him if Kensa was brought to justice.

Even as Tom brooded over what lay ahead, the wild journey ended with startling suddenness.

They found themselves on a wide, well-trodden road that led to the high gates of a walled city. Tom had visited this place many Quests ago when he had rescued Queen Romaine from the Wasp Beast, Vespick. This was Meaton, Kayonia's capital city, a bustling place surrounded by fields of waving golden corn.

Silver whined, lifting his muzzle and sniffing the air.

"Can you smell that terrible stench?" said Tom.

Elenna nodded, wrinkling her nose. "It's awful!"

Tom turned in the saddle, almost
overwhelmed by the foul stink.
"Look," he said, pointing to fields
where the corn was withering and

dying. "Why are the crops rotting?"

"The ground is so wet," said Elenna.

Tom could see that she was right. All around them, the earth was unpleasantly dank and slimy. It was almost like a marsh. He peered ahead. "What happened there?"

Close by the city gates, Tom saw that a section of the wall had collapsed. Men and women swarmed among the rubble, struggling to put together wooden scaffolding, presumably to prevent more of the wall from tumbling down.

Tom drew a rolled parchment map from Storm's saddlebag. He unrolled it and examined the extraordinary map of the three kingdoms. It was like no other map. It floated above the parchment, a tiny but exact replica of the real world. Mountains thrust up, forests rustled and rivers ran in rippling blue curves. Tom saw the town of Meaton in the center, the spires of Queen Romaine's castle jutting up like needles.

"This is wrong," Tom said. "According to this map, the Marshlands should be miles away from Meaton." He looked up again, staring more closely at the city. There were places where the cornfields had been entirely swamped by the creeping marsh. Fingers of slithering green bog were even crawling up to the walls of the city in some places.

"It must be the marsh that weakened the wall," said Elenna.

"This has to be the work of Kensa's Beasts!" Tom said grimly. "We have to do something before the whole of Meaton sinks into the marsh." He gently nudged Storm's sides with his heels. "Let's go to Queen Romaine – she'll help us track the Beast and put this right."

Storm moved forwards, lifting his hooves high to get them clear of the clinging mud. But even as they passed through the gates, Tom heard a frantic cry. The oozing ground was giving way beneath a tall, spindly construction of scaffold-poles.

People scattered as the structure came crashing down.

"Help me!"

Tom saw a man dangling by his fingers from the top of the wall. He was slipping.

Tom let out a gasp of alarm. *If he falls from that height, he'll be killed!*

CHAPTER TWO

A CEILING OF FANGS

"I have to help him!" cried Tom, jumping down from Storm's back and racing towards the crumbling wall. He spotted a wagon nearby, loaded with rotten corn stalks.

"Quickly," he called to the men and women standing nearby. "Bring the wagon up under the wall."

Elenna ran up as Tom and a small

group of people began to push the wagon across the wet ground. Just as they shoved it into place, the hanging man cried out and fell, crashing into the stalks with a squelch. Elenna clambered into the wagon and helped him off. He stood in front of Tom, shaking and covered with mouldy vegetation.

"Thank you," he gasped. Then his eyes widened. "I know you! You're the boy who saved us from Vespick."

An older man shuffled up. "We'll need more than a boy with a toy sword and tattered shield to help us from this curse," he muttered.

Tom looked at the frightened old man. He knew that it was the presence of a Beast that was warping the land, but he said nothing. The old man's comment about his tattered shield reminded Tom that the six tokens he had won on his very first Quest were lost to him now – they had withered and turned brown as a punishment when he had interrupted Aduro's trial. And his jewelled belt was gone, too. The only magic he had left now was the strength given to him by the suit of Golden Armour in King Hugo's castle, and the red jewel of Torgor that allowed him to communicate with Beasts.

With most of his powers gone, Tom knew that he'd need all of his courage and determination to defeat Kensa's Beasts. That, and the six coloured crystal orbs that he'd retrieved from the sorceress – the Lightning Tokens.

Tom and Elenna went back to where Storm and Silver were waiting. Tom took the horse's reins and they made their way through the sinking city towards the Queen's castle. The oozy marshland had turned the thoroughfares into stinking bogs. It had eaten away at the foundations of many houses so that they stood at strange angles, their roofs caved in.

Everywhere they went, they saw the wretched people of the city, either trying to shore up their tilting homes, or plodding through the muck with their belongings piled onto carts and wagons.

One of the people stared up at Tom and Elenna. "Why have you come here?" he cried. "There are earthquakes night and day! We must all leave before we are killed."

At last they reached the castle of Queen Romaine, which was built on higher ground, beyond the reach of the swamp. Its moat was empty save for a layer of green slime at the bottom.

A guard recognized Tom and Elenna and ushered them into the presence of the Queen, while Silver and Storm were taken to stables for food and shelter. Tom was shocked by the change in Queen Romaine. She was

slumped in her throne, her face pale
and drawn.

"Welcome," she said, attempting
a weak smile. "I am glad to see you
again, my friends, even at such a
terrible time. What brings you back
to Meaton?"

"A new threat has come to Kayonia,
Your Majesty," said Tom. "Remember

what you told me the last time we met? You said I could ask anything of you, and you would help."

Queen Romaine nodded wearily. "What do you need?"

"Some soldiers to help me fight a new Beast," Tom told her.

"You shall have them," said the Queen. "But in the meantime, you must stay the night."

"There isn't time," said Elenna.

"Some small refreshments, then," said the Queen, gesturing to a servant. "Stew to warm you while soldiers are gathered."

A small table was set up by the throne, and Tom and Elenna tucked into the hot stew. As they ate, Queen Romaine watched them carefully.

Elenna yawned. "I think a full stomach has made me sleepy."

Tom also felt strangely heavy and weary. He could hardly keep his eyes open. *I'm going to need some rest before I can fight another Beast*, he thought.

"There are comfortable beds in the south wing," said the Queen. "My servant will show you the way."

"The south wing, Your Majesty?" said the servant.

The Queen nodded. "Show them to the finest quarters!"

Tom felt too exhausted to argue as the servant led them from the throne room.

They were taken to separate rooms on opposite sides of a corridor. Tom heard the clatter of claws as he entered his room. He turned to see Silver loping along the corridor, whining uneasily. He settled down, laying between their doors.

"Good boy," Tom heard Elenna say through a huge yawn. "Are you here to keep watch?"

Without even bothering to remove his sword and shield, Tom sank down onto the grand four-poster bed. He gazed sleepily up at the heavy velvet canopy that hung above him. The feather mattress folded around his body, warm and deep.

I'll just close my eyes for a little while, he thought.

Creak! Tom's eyes snapped open in the deep gloom. Something strange was happening. He tried to sit up but he was unable to move. He struggled to lift an arm. It was useless! His eyes rolled from side to side.

He tried to call out, but his jaw was locked.

The canopy of the bed had sprouted

long curved spikes, like the fangs of a dragon. That was where the creaking sound had come from! The velvet canopy dropped slowly towards him

on some kind of clanking mechanism. He struggled to get up, but his body felt as heavy as lead. *How was this possible?* Desperately, he thought back, remembering the way Romaine had watched him eat.

The food! he thought. *The stew the Queen gave us was drugged!*

CHAPTER THREE

SPIKES AND SMOKE

Tom felt cold sweat running down his face as the deadly spikes dropped further. Fighting the effects of the drugged stew, he tried desperately to move as the cruel barbs descended. But his whole body was rigid and numb. He could not even feel the mattress that he was lying on.

Think, Tom!

Then he had a flash of hope. The

effects of the stew prevented him from being able to talk or shout, but he could still think.

And he still had Torgor's ruby, which allowed him to speak to Beasts. And during Tom's Quest in Seraph, evil magic had briefly turned Silver into a Beast...

It has to be worth a try.

Tom focused his thoughts on Silver, the sweat pouring off him as he fought to let the faithful wolf know what was happening.

Help me, Silver!

It was hard to concentrate. The grinding noise was getting louder and the spikes were horribly close. Tom looked up and saw that the sharp point of one of them was aimed right at his eye.

There was no sign of Silver. The

power of the jewel hadn't worked.

I can't die like this, Tom thought desperately. *I won't!*

Just as Tom was about to give up hope, he heard the scrabble of claws on the floor, Silver's teeth closed around his sleeve and Tom felt himself dragged off the bed. A spike tore through his trouser leg.

Tom heard the crack and crunch of wood as the bed was crushed under the weight of the mechanism.

That could have been me! he thought, as he lay gasping for breath.

Silver gently butted him with his muzzle, then pulled at him with his paws.

"I…can't…move…" gasped Tom. The wolf caught hold of his collar and dragged him towards a small side-table that stood against the wall. There was a jug on the table. Using every last shred of willpower, Tom managed to fling an arm out. His hand hit the table and the jug fell over, sending a gush of cold water over his face.

Tom's arms and legs twitched as life flooded back into his body. "I did it!" he spluttered, spitting out water as he sat up.

Silver gave a yelp of joy.

"Clever boy," Tom said, stretching his stiff limbs and patting the wolf's flank. He stood up, feeling a little shaky and woozy still. What had Queen Romaine been thinking to put him in such a dangerous room?

Silver turned, sniffing the air. He yelped and ran into the corridor.

Elenna! Tom thought.

He saw Silver scrabble frantically at her door, as thin wisps of smoke seeped out from underneath. Elenna was in danger. Tom staggered over to the door, his legs still unsteady, his head floating from the effects of the drugged food.

Silver leapt at the door, desperately trying to force it open. But the handle was stuck. Tom added his own weight, shouldering up hard against the oak panels.

The door burst open and a dense cloud of smoke billowed into Tom's face. He could hear his friend choking as he stumbled about blindly, trying to find her bed. He hit a window. Pulling his shield off his back, he smashed the glass, allowing the smoke to escape.

He could now see that the smoke was coming from a fireplace. He ran across the room to where Elenna was lying on the bed, coughing badly. Silver was at her side, as though standing guard.

Tom picked up a jug of water by her bedside and poured it over her face. "We've been drugged," he said.

Elenna gasped and spat out the water, her limbs quivering as she regained control of them. Hooking a hand under her arm, Tom led her into the corridor.

"The chimney must be blocked," Elenna gasped. "I could have suffocated."

"It was no accident," Tom said grimly. "Come on, we need to speak to the queen!"

With Silver loping along at their side, Tom and Elenna made their way through the deserted castle to the throne room. Tom was fully recovered now and filled with anger at what the queen had done to them. Despite the lateness of the hour, they found Romaine wide-awake, pacing back and forth.

She gave them a shocked look as they entered.

Tom drew his sword. "Why did you try to kill us?"

"I did not," exclaimed the queen. "What are you saying?"

"Spikes and smoke," said Tom angrily. "Don't pretend you have no idea what I'm talking about."

The queen's face filled with anguish. "The south wing of the palace was built by a wicked ancestor of mine." She bowed her head, looking ashamed. "He used it to kill his enemies. I have never done such a thing before."

"Then why do it now?" demanded Elenna.

"Because we forced her to," snarled a cruel voice from behind them. Tom spun around. The doorway was blocked by a band of burly, armed men. Silver growled.

Tom gasped in shock, recognizing the pirates' ragged clothing and their Beast-skull tattoos. *Sanpao's crew!*

One of the pirates stepped forwards,

a curved scimitar in his hand. "The captain sends his fondest greetings to you both," he growled. "He only wishes he could be here…" Cruel light ignited in his eyes. "…to see you die!"

With fearsome roars, the pirates drew their weapons and charged forwards.

CHAPTER FOUR

BATTLE FOR THE THRONE ROOM

Tom darted under the leading pirate's scything sword and used his shield to strike the brute in the stomach.

An unhappy thought flashed through Tom's mind as the pirate doubled over with a gasp. *My shield was so much more powerful before the magic tokens withered away.*

Tom pushed the winded pirate back

and then swung his sword at a second
villain, who backed away and collided
with another. Both of them tumbled
to the floor. Tom glimpsed Queen
Romaine cowering against the wall
with a look of horror on her face.

Two more of the pirates stumbled
over their fallen comrades while the

sixth and last pirate threw himself aside with a howl as one of Elenna's arrows skimmed past him and slammed into the doorframe.

Silver leapt forwards, sinking his teeth into the arm of a fallen pirate, shaking it until the scimitar fell out of his hand.

"Regroup!" Tom shouted to his companions, leading them deeper into the throne room. "Shoot from cover," he called to Elenna, who dived behind the queen's throne and began loosing arrows in rapid succession.

The pirates staggered to their feet, their faces red with wrath, their scimitars gleaming in the candlelight as they scattered to avoid Elenna's shots. Tom ran to a long table and jumped up onto it. Two of the biggest pirates chased after him, swiping their swords at his legs. Tom leapt above the blades and jabbed out his own, forcing the pirates to draw back as he sprang from the end of the table onto a long oak cabinet. The bellowing pirates hurtled after him.

Tom glimpsed Silver, leaping back into the fray, trapping a pirate in one corner. The unarmed sea-bandit already had bite wounds on his arms.

The other two pirates were jumping from side to side to avoid Elenna's arrows as they tried in vain to approach the throne.

"She's only a girl!" roared one of them, ducking as an arrow skimmed past his ear. "Don't just stand there, you fool! Get her!"

The other threw himself flat as another shaft whistled over his head.

"Why me?" he shouted back. "You're closer. You get her!"

Tom twisted around on the cabinet, and kicked a large metal candlestick into the face of one of the pirates chasing him. The man tumbled to the ground, clutching his bleeding nose. Tom jumped down on top of him, kicking the scimitar clear and sending it spinning through the air.

The other pirate came at him like an

enraged bull. Tom dodged aside and heard the man's blade slash a long ragged tear down a wall tapestry. He leaped up and snatched at the top of the thick cloth, ripping it from its rail so that it fell in heavy folds over the two pirates. He then slammed the flat of his sword down on their skulls. The two struggling shapes went limp.

He turned and flung his shield through the air. It bounced off the last pirate's forehead, toppling him backwards to crash to the floor, out cold.

"Well done, Elenna," Tom shouted. "And you, Silver. Let's find something to tie them up with."

He stepped forwards, but a cry from Elenna made him spin around. "Behind you!"

One of the pirates had wriggled out

from beneath the tapestry and was lunging for him with a dagger. But before the villain could stab Tom, Queen Romaine ran up behind him, and felled him with a blow from a candlestick.

It wasn't long before all five of the pirates were lying on the floor, safely bound with rope.

The queen wrung her hands in anguish. "I had no choice but to betray you," she groaned. "They kidnapped my daughter, Esmeralda. They threatened to hang her from the mast of their ship."

"The filthy cowards," Tom snarled, taking out a fragment of magic mirror that King Hugo had given him. "This has the power to help me find people," he explained to the queen. "Do you have a picture of Esmeralda?"

The queen opened a locket that hung around her neck. Tom looked at the picture of the princess. She was wearing a green riding cloak and her pale face was framed by long, corn-yellow hair. Tom fixed the princess's face in his mind, then stared into the mirror, concentrating hard. An image appeared in the glass. It was a dark ship's hold. A lantern swung from a low rafter. The princess was huddled in a grimy corner among coils of tarred rope. Her ankles and wrists were bound tight, but there was a defiant look in her eyes.

"I see her," Tom said. "She's tied up, but she doesn't seem to be hurt."

"She'll be hurt enough when Sanpao learns of what happened here!" one of the pirates snarled.

"You won't be the ones to tell him,"

snapped Queen Romaine angrily. She called for servants. "Take these scoundrels to my deepest dungeons."

As the pirates were being dragged away, there came a loud rumbling noise and Tom had to steady himself as the whole castle seemed to shake. From a window he saw one of the towers collapse into rubble.

"The entire city will be in ruins if nothing is done," cried Queen Romaine. "And with every quake the marsh creeps closer." She looked at Tom. "I'm sorry, all my soldiers will be needed to help the suffering folk of Meaton."

Her eyes then lit up. "But there is something else I can do to aid you in your Quest. Something even better than soldiers."

CHAPTER FIVE

THE BLINDING FOG

Queen Romaine led Tom and Elenna down many flights of stone steps into the deepest vaults of the palace. She held a blazing torch in her hand and the light gleamed on the walls as they passed. Silver walked with them, sniffing the air and growling uncertainly.

She won't betray us again, Tom thought. *Not now that she knows we'll do everything we can to help free her daughter.*

They came at last to a great iron door. "This is the Royal Armoury," said the queen, leading them in by torchlight. The flames glimmered on swords and shields and plate armour as she moved through the long high-vaulted room.

She opened the lid to a large wooden chest. Something lay within, wrapped in cloth. Very carefully, the queen unwrapped the object. For a moment, Tom thought it was a sheet of thin glass, but then, as Romaine held it up in the torchlight, he realized what she was holding.

"Vespick's wing!" he exclaimed, his mind flooding with memories of his deadly aerial battle with the terrible Wasp Queen.

"It was discovered when an earthquake created a split in the bottom of the castle moat and the water drained away," the queen explained. "I had it put here for safe-keeping, but I know such a token can only belong to a warrior like you."

Tom took the wing from her. It was slender and light, but he could feel that

it was also very strong.

"Be careful," warned Elenna.
"Remember, it came from an Evil
Beast."

"I don't think it can harm us," said
Tom. He quickly tied a strap around the

wing and looped it over his shoulder.

Since my own shield has lost its magic, maybe Vespick's wing will help me in battle, he thought.

"Thank you," he said to the queen. "Now we must be on our way." He took out the parchment map and unrolled it as Elenna leant close with a torch. The magical three-dimensional map glowed in the light. A clear path wound its way out of the palace towards the marshlands.

"I wish it had led anywhere but there," murmured Elenna. "Those marshes could suck us to our deaths before we ever meet the Beast."

"There's no other choice," said Tom, as a name appeared on the map, right in the middle of the marsh.

Vigrash.

Now they had a clear path before

them, there was no time to lose. They
made their way up to the stables to
fetch Storm. They could see that the
horse had been well looked after, but
he reared up on his hind legs and
neighed loudly, delighted to see his
friends again and eager to be off.

"You have my eternal gratitude for
what you are about to do," said Queen
Romaine.

"We will find the princess," said Tom,
as he and Elenna climbed into the
saddle.

Queen Romaine bid them good luck
before they left the palace and cantered
away through the devastated city of
Meaton.

They rode through the gates and
entered the marsh. As they travelled
on, a thick greenish fog rose all around
them, coating their clothes and their

skin with oily slime and filling their nostrils with a foul stink.

"Is it me, or has the smell got worse?" muttered Elenna, her hand over her mouth and nose.

"I think we're heading into the heart of all this foulness," Tom replied.

Silver sniffed the air and shook his head, his paws thick with mud. But Storm was finding the going even harder. He was fetlock-deep in the clinging ooze, and he stumbled, lifting his hooves high as he fought for solid ground.

"We're too heavy," said Tom. He and Elenna jumped down, their feet splashing in the mire. Now they were no longer on Storm's back, the fog wrapped around them in a chilly embrace.

Tom led Storm on into the deeps of

the marsh, squinting to see through the thickening fog. He felt dizzy. He stumbled and had to clutch at Storm's reins to stay on his feet.

"Are you all right?" Elenna asked anxiously, coming to his side.

"I think Queen Romaine's potion has not fully worn off," Tom told her.

"Perhaps we should rest for a while?" Elenna suggested.

"No!" Tom said firmly. "There's no time. We must keep searching for Vigrash. And don't forget Princess Esmeralda needs our help as well. No matter how hard it gets, no matter how hopeless it seems – while there's blood in my veins, I will not give up!"

His fingers moved to the grey pebble that hung around his neck. It was a gift from Daltec, Aduro's apprentice. He had told Tom that it would glow red if Kensa or Sanpao were close by. For the moment, the pebble was still grey.

Tom's fingers instinctively moved to his sword hilt when a high, wailing screech rent the air.

"What was that?" he asked, peering into the thick mist.

"It sounded like a man," said Elenna, an arrow to her bow as she tried to peer through the green fog.

"Help!" cried a despairing voice.

Then there was a splash and a horrible sucking noise.

The voice called again, but this time it was cut off short with desperate gurgling sounds.

"Someone's out there," Tom gasped. "And I think they're drowning."

CHAPTER SIX

THE MAD MAN OF THE MARSH

Tom and Elenna ran side by side into the mist, following the sounds of thrashing and splashing. Silver loped ahead, howling loudly, helping to guide them.

Plunging through the fog, Tom saw a man, waist deep in the bog. His clothes were torn and his face and hair were spattered with mud.

Tom threw himself onto the ground, reaching for the man.

"I'm here," he called. "Take my hand."

The man's wide, bloodshot eyes fixed on him. His arm swiped feebly, but he was too far away. Tom edged forwards, careful not to go too far.

"Hold my legs," he called to Elenna, feeling her grab his ankles as he crawled towards the man. At last he was close enough to take a handful of the man's tattered clothing.

Calling on all the strength given to him by the Golden Armour in King Hugo's armoury, he dragged the man out of the swamp and onto firmer ground. The man threw his arms around Tom's knees, clinging on.

Silver sniffed him, but backed off as the man gave a start and yelped

in fear. "Don't hurt me," he cried pitifully.

"We won't," said Elenna, helping the cowering man to his feet. "You're safe now."

"Safe?" screeched the man, staring madly from one to the other. "Not safe. Never safe again." He crouched, peering anxiously at the sky.

"Who are you, sir?" asked Tom.

The man stared at him. "I'm Kurt that Rat Catcher,' he said. "The rats knew about the flying monster. It was a lion. Or an eagle." He nodded wildly. "Yes, the eagle was a lion. Or maybe the lion was an eagle." He gave a gurgle of mad laughter. "Who can say?"

"Has he lost his mind?" Elenna whispered to Tom.

"I'm not sure," Tom muttered back, gazing upwards. "Perhaps he caught a glimpse of Vigrash. Who knows what the next Beast might look like?" He looked at the terrified man. "We should try to get him to safe ground before we do anything else," he said.

"Safe ground?" muttered Kurt, wringing his hands. "There's no such thing anymore. There's no way out of the marsh. We'll have to scurry like rats through the mud until the monster comes swooping down to swallow us whole. Just like rats." He broke into another peal of laughter. "We'll be left for dead in the marshes, yes we will. Torn to shreds and gobbled up."

"That's enough of such talk," said Tom sternly. "Whatever you saw, we'll protect you from it."

Kurt sank to his knees, his eyes turned upwards, one arm thrusting into the air. "Here it comes," he groaned. "It's coming to eat us."

Storm came trotting out of the mist, his eyes rolling, snorting and pawing the soft ground in alarm. Silver's yellow eyes stared upwards into the swirling green mist.

"They sense something," Elenna

murmured, her hands quickly fitting an arrow to her bow.

"It's here..." whispered Kurt.

Tom heard the sound of heavy wing beats above. He drew his sword and pulled himself loose from the crouching man. Another wave of dizziness made him stumble for a moment as the steady beating of the wings grew louder. He craned his neck to scan the sky, desperately trying to work out where the noise was coming from.

Then, a patch of fog was swept aside and Tom was finally able to see the Beast hovering above him, supported by wide, arching black wings. It had the body and hide of a great, muscular golden lion but the head of a bird of prey with fierce black eyes and a long curved beak.

"Vigrash!" Tom breathed,
tightening his grip on his sword.
The Beast hovered for a moment

or two, then folded her wings and plummeted downwards, her lion claws reaching out, wicked beak gaping wide. She gave a cry that was as booming as a roar and as shrill as a shrieking eagle.

"Get down!" Tom shouted. Elenna flung herself onto her belly as the screeching Beast swept overhead. Tom jabbed upwards with his sword, the blade clanging on an unsheathed claw.

Vigrash turned in the air, her wings spreading as she swept over Tom's head. A trailing edge of her wing caught Storm in the side. With a neigh of pain and fear, the stallion was flung off his hooves.

"Storm!" Tom shouted, running towards his horse, who was kicking his legs, his eyes filled with panic, as Vigrash rose into the air.

Tom realized they were in for the fight of their lives.

CHAPTER SEVEN

CERTAIN DEATH

Tom snatched at Storm's reins and pulled, giving the fallen horse the extra boost he needed to clamber shakily to his hooves.

But no sooner was Storm upright than the Beast came swooping down again, lion claws raking and beak open wide in an ear-splitting screech. Tom swung his sword high.

Vigrash rose on flapping wings.

Tom reeled from the stink created by each beat – foul as the marsh was, the stench given off by the Beast was far worse. Kurt lay squirming in the mud, moaning feebly with his hands covering his eyes.

"Keep away, you monster!" Tom heard Elenna shout. There was the twang of a bow-string and the dull thud of an arrow burying deep into Vigrash's side.

"Nice shooting, Elenna!" Tom called.

The Beast let out a shriek of anger, her wings cupping the air as she rose higher. But the arrow seemed to have enraged rather than wounded Vigrash, who twisted her head around and easily tore the arrow loose with her beak.

"You can't kill it," cackled Kurt, stumbling to his feet but cowering down with his arms over his head. "We must run and hide."

"No!" shouted Tom. "Running is the worst thing we can do." Unless he stood and fought, they would be easy prey – he could already imagine those long curved claws tearing into their backs as they fled. And with the queen's poison still flowing in his veins, he didn't trust himself to be able to run without stumbling and making himself an even easier target.

The maddened Beast plunged at them again. Tom stared in horror into the red depths of her cavernous throat and felt the terrible wind of her sickening breath. He swung wildly with his sword, only just managing to fend off the razor-sharp beak. He ducked low as the monster dived. Elenna dropped onto her face as the claws tore the air a fraction above her back.

Silver leapt high, his jaws snapping, but the edge of a black wing sent him spinning. The Beast turned in the air, snatching for Storm. Whinnying in fear, Tom's horse skittered away, plunging into the mist.

Vigrash let out a screech as she turned from the horse. Her glassy black eyes fixed on Tom, almost as though she knew he was her most dangerous enemy.

Tom saw something from the corner of his eye. When Storm had fallen, the bag with the six lightning tokens had come loose from his saddle. It was lying there in the ooze.

As the Beast sped towards him, Tom crouched and then sprang, stabbing at his enemy's eagle-head. Vigrash twisted in mid-air, rising high to avoid the sharp blade. With the space clear, Tom flung himself towards the saddlebag, curling into a roll, his ears filled with the terrible screeching.

He grabbed the bag, staggering to his feet and running as best he could over the soft ground.

I must draw the Beast away from the others long enough to use one of the lightning tokens against her.

"Tom, be careful!" he heard Elenna call.

As he ran, he snatched an orb from the bag. It was glassy and strangely heavy with a tiny bolt of red lightning at its heart. The tokens had not failed him in the past, and he felt sure that this one would help to bring about Vigrash's downfall.

He ran unsteadily through the mist until he found firmer, higher ground. Then he turned, brandishing his sword.

"I'm Avantia's Master of the Beasts," he cried. "Vigrash, while there's blood in my veins, I'll find a way to defeat you!"

The Beast hurtled towards him, her furious keening filling the air. Tom stood firm, his sword ready and the orb clutched in his hand.

But a wave of dizziness swept over him again. The world spun around him and he dropped to one knee, as if pushed to the ground by the hand of a Beast.

No! Not now!

He heard the hurricane rush of wings above him. Claws dug into his tunic, piercing his skin and making him cry out with pain. A moment later he was lifted bodily from the ground as Vigrash's wings beat the air with tremendous power.

"No!" he let out a cry as the lightning orb slipped from his fingers.

His head swam as the Beast hoisted him up high into the air. He tried to twist around and fight back, but he couldn't land a clean blow with his sword.

He heard Elenna's voice below him.
"Tom! Try to fight free."

I can't, he thought. *I'm helpless!*

Higher and higher the Beast flew
– and suddenly Tom realized what

Vigrash meant to do. She would carry him high into the air, and then she would let him fall. Without the power of Arcta's eagle feather, he'd plunge to his death!

But a sudden hope ignited in Tom's heart. Perhaps if he used Torgor's ruby, he could persuade her to let him live. Tom pushed his fear aside and concentrated on getting a message to the Beast.

Vigrash – can you hear me? We needn't be enemies. Maybe we can—

Tom's thoughts were interrupted by terrible images of anger and fear, rampaging through his mind. Somehow, he knew that these were the Beast's own memories.

Memories involving Tom's father.

In his mind's eye, Tom saw Taladon standing over Vigrash as the Beast sank into mire. The Beast was shrieking in agony and dread. One of its wings looked broken and mangled. But Taladon was doing nothing to help – in fact he was laughing as the Beast struggled.

Tom couldn't understand what he was seeing.

Why is my father allowing a Beast to suffer? Even an Evil Beast deserves better than that.

As the images faded, Tom realized with a sickening jolt that Vigrash somehow sensed that he was the son of the man who had tormented her.

There will be no chance of me persuading this Beast to let me live.

Vigrash hovered, high in the sky. Tom stared down – the marsh was just a greenish blur far, far below.

The Beast sent a final dreadful

thought into Tom's mind

The son of Taladon must die!

Then, with an ear-splitting shriek, she released him.

Tom fell, tumbling helplessly to his certain death.

CHAPTER EIGHT

FOOD FOR THE BEAST

Tom flailed through the air, his ears filled with the triumphant caws of Vigrash. The mist-covered marshes rushed up towards him. There was nothing he could do to save himself.

But then he felt a vibration at his back.

Vespick's wing!

He had almost forgotten it was

there, but now it seemed to be struggling to get loose. In desperation, Tom pulled the glassy wing off his back, holding it above his head in both hands.

Immediately, he felt the speed of his fall slow down. He hung beneath the wing, almost gliding, sweeping down feet first into the thick mist.

Tom bent his knees, preparing to

hit the ground as he cut through the fog at an angle. He crashed down in deep muddy water. A huge spurt of brown slime gushed up into the air as he landed. But he was alive and uninjured. The wing had saved him!

Spattered all over with mud, he waded in search of firmer ground. But he heard the dreadful rush of wings as the shadow of the Beast swept over him. Vigrash was coming.

Tom swung his sword high as the Beast swooped. The blade missed, but it sprayed liquid mud over Vigrash's head and wings. The Beast shot up into the air with a shriek of rage.

Tom stared in surprise. Why had she not attacked? He saw Vigrash hovering above him, her neck straining around and her long thin tongue licking at the mud on her wings.

"So, you do have a weakness," Tom muttered to himself. "You have the flight of a bird, but a cat's hatred of getting dirty." Or perhaps the Beast was cleaning herself because she knew that she would be unable to fly if her wings were clogged with filth. Either way, it gave Tom new hope.

"Elenna! Storm! Silver!" Tom shouted as he waded through the thick mud.

"Here!" he heard Elenna call.

He turned and stumbled through the knee-high mud towards the sound of her voice. But the vision of his father still troubled him. It made no sense. Taladon had been the noble Master of the Beasts – he should never have taken pleasure when a Beast was suffering.

Tom saw Storm through the mist.

Elenna and Silver and Kurt were with the horse. He was relieved that the frightened stallion had returned, and he used Storm's dangling reins to help pull himself up out of the mud and onto firmer ground.

"I lost the lightning token," he gasped. "But I think I know how we can get Kurt to safety." He stooped and scooped up a handful of thick mud. "We'll head for the city," he explained. "If Vigrash comes close, throw mud at her."

Elenna stared at him in surprise. "Are you sure?" she asked.

Tom nodded. "Trust me," he said. "If we can clog up the Beast's feathers with mud, I think we might be able to stop her from flying."

No sooner had Tom spoken than he heard the familiar, terrible screeching of the Beast.

"Get ready!" he said to his companions.

Gathering up handfuls of mud, Tom led Elenna and Kurt away from the two animals and onto a hump of higher, drier land. "Stand back to back," he told Elenna as the Beast's hissing shrieks grew louder. "Kurt – get between us. We'll protect you."

"She's coming!" Elenna shouted, hurling mud. Tom spun around, seeing Vigrash gliding low through the mist. He threw two handfuls of mud at the Beast, then crouched to pick up more.

Vigrash turned away, circling them, squawking furiously as the mud clung to her wings. Elenna was as quick with the mud missiles as she was with her arrows. Clump after clump

of sodden earth flew from her hands,
spattering the Beast's wings, drawing
even more enraged screeches from
her throat.

Tom wiped his hands clean and
took out the map to check the path
back to Meaton. Then he rolled it up
and pushed it back into his tunic.

"Follow me," he said, picking up more mud and throwing it to keep Vigrash at bay.

As he led them to the edge of the marsh, Tom noticed that when Vigrash swept away to try and avoid the mud-missiles, she almost always veered off to the left. He kept that thought in his mind as they struggled slowly on.

"My rat-sack!" said Kurt, pointing to a squirming brown bag that lay in the mud. "Some of the rats must have climbed back inside. There's food in there," he continued. "I always bait my traps with tasty morsels."

Tom stared at him, a plan forming in his mind.

"Bait!" he said, looking at Elenna. "That's what we need to bring Vigrash down out of the sky."

"I'll be the bait," Elenna offered.

"Are you sure?" Tom asked.

Elenna gave a brave smile. "Just so long as Beast bait doesn't become Beast food," she said.

While I'm alive, that will never happen! thought Tom.

CHAPTER NINE

SAVING THE BEAST

"We need to split up," Tom said.
"Kurt, listen to me and try to think
straight. Take Storm's reins, go to that
clump of tall reeds and try to keep
out of sight. I need you to be strong."
He rested his hand on Silver's head,
pointing into the distance. "Go with
them, boy. Protect them. Quickly
now!"

Kurt scuttled off with the two

animals. The swirling mist rustled the reeds as the three of them faded from sight.

Elenna ran to a patch of higher ground while Tom crouched close by, clutching the writhing sack of rats. "I'm here!" Elenna called to the Beast, lifting her arms into the air. "I'm waiting for you."

Vigrash came with a screech and a rush, floating through the mist on spread wings, claws glinting and beak snapping.

Elenna slung two handfuls of mud at the Beast. Vigrash's fur bristled as she swerved away from Elenna to the left. Tom was ready. He sprang up. The power of his golden leg armour gave him the boost he needed to leap onto the Beast's broad back. He could feel Vigrash's powerful muscles bunching under him, and his nostrils were full of her dreadful stench.

Screaming with rage, Vigrash jerked upwards, twisting her body as she fought to throw Tom off. But Tom clung onto her rough fur with one hand as he upended the bag of rats.

The creatures swarmed over the Beast, clinging on with their sharp little claws, climbing up Vigrash's neck and along her wings. Vigrash

arched her back, to try and bite at the rats. Some fell as the Beast rose swiftly above the mists, and a few clung painfully to Tom's arms and legs, but the rest were swarming over Vigrash, who shrieked with anger and panic.

As the Beast tried to rid herself of the crawling vermin, her wings lost rhythm and she began losing height. Still twisting and turning desperately and letting out screech after screech, Vigrash plunged down into the mist. Tom clutched at her fur as he was thrown violently from side to side.

Down below, a wide patch of greenish swamp became visible through the mist. Tom leapt from the Beast's back at the very last moment, hurling himself onto a hump of grass as Vigrash plunged into deep, clinging mud.

Tom landed well, quickly leaping to his feet to see Vigrash thrashing wildly in the swamp. Her wings flailed, spraying fountains of slime in all directions. The rats were swimming, fleeing the huge Beast as it sank deeper. Vigrash's neck strained up as her body disappeared.

As the Beast's huge bird-head

turned towards Tom, their eyes met. Vigrash looked terrified. She was sinking fast and Tom felt a twinge of sympathy for his enemy as she fought not to drown.

Tom stared down at the doomed Beast, wishing there was something he could do to help her. He heard squelching steps behind him and turned to see Elenna and Kurt and the two animals approaching.

Kurt gawped at the Beast with wide, frightened eyes.

"She can't do us any harm now," Tom told him. "The poor creature is helpless."

As they watched, the struggling Beast sank further, so that only her shoulders, head, and the tips of her bedraggled wings were visible above the swamp.

Kurt began to stamp and point. "Let her drown!" he shouted triumphantly.

Tom shook his head, remembering the vision of Taladon mocking the wretched Beast. "This is no way to treat a living creature," he muttered. "Not even an Evil Beast."

He ran to where Storm was standing and took a rope from one of the saddlebags. Looping it into a lasso, he ran to the very edge of the firm ground.

"Tom, are you sure about this?" Elenna asked. "Vigrash would never show you such compassion."

Tom nodded. "I must," he said. "It would be wrong to let her suffer." He swung the rope around his head a few times then flung it towards the swamp.

Vigrash snapped at it with her beak.

"That's it!" Tom shouted, sure that the Beast would realize that he was trying to help despite the fact she could not understand his words. "Hold on, we're going to pull you out."

"Not I!" shouted Kurt. "You two must be mad."

Tom turned fiercely on him. "You *will* help," he said.

Cowed by Tom's anger, Kurt joined Elenna on the rope and they all hauled on it while Vigrash held it tightly in her beak. Very slowly, the Beast was dragged towards dry land. Her front paws emerged, dripping with slime. Her wings, black with caked mud, heaved uselessly.

"Harder!" Tom said between gritted teeth. The Beast was very heavy and the bog clung mercilessly to her. But at last, using every ounce of strength, they managed to haul Vigrash up onto dry ground.

She lay there, gasping for breath, her wings splayed feebly on the ground, her chest rising and falling rapidly.

"You're safe now," Tom told Kurt. "Can you find your way back to Meaton from here?"

"Yes," said Kurt. He felt in a pocket. "I found something in the reeds – maybe it belongs to you?"

He held out the glassy token with the tiny red fork of lightning at its heart.

"I don't think I'll be needing it," Tom began, but his words were drowned out by a frightened shout from Elenna.

"Look out, Tom!"

He spun around to see Vigrash rearing up, her eyes filled with malice. The Beast's wings might be useless, but her claws were still deadly as they came raking down towards him. He leaped back at the last moment, and the deadly curved blades whistled past.

Tom snatched the Lightning Token out of Kurt's hand and flung it with all his strength. But he judged the throw badly and the orb sailed over the Beast's head, missing it completely.

Vigrash rose up in her hind legs, her beak wide.

Once more the Beast's voice sounded loud within his head.

The Son of Taladon must die!

Tom fell back, realizing that his compassion may have doomed them all.

CHAPTER TEN

BLOOD RED SAILS

As Tom stumbled back, he heard a whizzing sound, closely followed by a loud smash and a burst of blinding light. He had to throw his arms up over his face to shield his eyes from the glare. But the flash had burned an image onto his eyelids and he could see exactly what had happened. Swift as the wind, Elenna had loosed an arrow, sending it over the Beast's

head and shattering the lightning
token into a thousand fragments,
releasing the dazzling burst of light.

Vigrash was gone. Tom had done
his duty, but his feeling of victory was
mixed with relief that he had not let
the Beast suffer as his father seemed
to have done.

When Tom's eyes cleared, nothing
of Vigrash remained except for paw
prints dug deep into the marsh. Tom
grasped the ruby and sent a final

thought to the Beast, hoping that she would hear him, wherever she was.

You fought well… Be at peace now.

His thoughts were interrupted by a whoop of joy from Kurt.

He turned. Elenna stood with her bow in her hands, a look of steely determination on her face.

"Thank you for saving me again," he told her, with a smile.

"You're welcome," she replied. A frown creased her forehead. "Vigrash wanted you dead, even after you tried to save her life."

"I know," said Tom. "When I used Torgor's ruby to try and communicate with the Beast, I was given a vision that my father taunted her once. The Beast somehow knew that I was Taladon's son."

"He taunted her?" Elenna asked in

a puzzled voice. "That doesn't sound like Taladon at all. Why would he do such a thing?"

"I don't know," Tom said quietly. He shook his head. "We should go back to Meaton. Queen Romaine will be glad of the good news."

Taking Kurt along with them, they picked their way carefully through the marsh. It wasn't long until they came to the city walls. Things seemed already to be changing there. The ground was less wet underfoot, and the foul stink had faded, as though the marsh were slowly draining away again.

"Now that Vigrash is gone, things are getting back to normal," Tom said as they made their way through the city.

Kurt stopped, shaking Elenna and Tom's hands.

"I must be about my business now,"
he said with a grin. "It's good to know
that heroes are prepared to save even
a lowly rat catcher like me." He spun
around, pointing at a black rat that
was scuttling down a grimy side-
street. "Aha! There's no rest for the
wicked!" Kurt cackled, racing off, his
rat-catching sack bouncing on his
shoulder. "Come to Kurt! There's
a good rat!"

Smiling, Elenna and Tom continued
towards the high castle. Queen
Romaine was waiting for them at the
gates, a hopeful look on her face.

"The Beast is defeated," Tom told
her. "The natural order of things will
return now."

"I feared I might never see you
again," she said, but her eyes darted
this way and that. "Have you not

found my daughter?"

Tom shook his head sadly. He was about to speak when he felt the pebble hanging around his neck suddenly become hot. He drew it out of his tunic and saw that it was glowing as bright as a ruby.

"Kensa must be close by," he muttered, his pulse quickening.

"There!" cried Elenna, pointing to the sky as a familiar, dreadful shape came gliding out of a bank of clouds.

It was Sanpao's flying pirate ship, soaring high above them with its blood-red sails billowing. Tom felt a stab of anger and loathing as the ship began descending towards them in wide spirals.

He drew his sword and brandished it in the air. "Face me in combat, you cowards!" he shouted.

As the ship sailed overhead, Silver growled and jumped up as though desperate to sink his fangs into each one of their enemies. Storm whickered and stomped at the ground.

The ship soared over the castle ramparts, the creak of its timbers and the snap of its sails loud in Tom's ears.

A pale, frightened face appeared over the rail.

"Esmeralda!" Queen Romaine shouted, reaching up with both arms.

"Mother," cried the princess. "Help me!"

Cruel faces stared down from either side of the terrified princess with vicious, merciless smiles on their faces. One was Kensa, her eyes as green as poison. The other was the darkly tattooed face of Sanpao the Pirate King, one of the most deadly foes Tom and Elenna had ever encountered.

"Return my child to me!" the
Queen demanded.

"I don't think so," shouted Sanpao.
"We enjoy her company too much to
do that, Your Majesty."

"Indeed we do," called Kensa. "In
fact, we love her so dearly, we think
we'll keep her!"

Tom pointed his sword at them, his blood boiling with anger. "No matter how far you run," he called, "I will find you. That's a promise!"

"I hope you do," Kensa called. "I have a wonderful death planned for you!"

"Sail away, my hearties!" Sanpao bellowed to his pirate crew. "We cannot linger here. We have great work to do!"

A few moments later, the ship turned about, sails catching the wind before it soared away. Soon, it was no more than a tiny dot.

Tom turned to the queen. "Do not fear for your daughter's life," he said grimly. "Kensa and Sanpao can try any dirty trick they can think of, but while there is blood in my veins, I will not give up my Quest!"

Join Tom on the next stage
of the Beast Quest when he meets

MIRKA
THE ICE HORSE

Win an exclusive
Beast Quest T-shirt and goody bag!

In every Beast Quest book the Beast Quest logo is hidden in one of the pictures. Find the logos in books 67 to 72 and make a note of which pages they appear on. Write the six page numbers on a postcard and send it in to us.

Each month we will draw one winner to receive a Beast Quest T-shirt and goody bag.

THE BEAST QUEST COMPETITION:
THE DARKEST HOUR
Orchard Books
338 Euston Road, London NW1 3BH
Australian readers should email:
childrens.books@hachette.com.au

New Zealand readers should write to:
Beast Quest Competition
4 Whetu Place, Mairangi Bay, Auckland, NZ
or email: childrensbooks@hachette.co.nz

Only one entry per child.
Final draw: January 2014

You can also enter this competition
via the Beast Quest website: www.beastquest.co.uk

Join the Quest,
Join the Tribe

www.beastquest.co.uk

Have you checked out the Beast Quest website?
It's the place to go for games, downloads, activities,
sneak previews and lots of fun!

You can read all about your favourite Beasts,
download free screensavers and desktop wallpapers
for your computer, and even challenge your friends
to a Beast Tournament.

Sign up to the newsletter at www.beastquest.co.uk
to receive exclusive extra content and the
opportunity to enter special members-only
competitions. We'll send you up-to-date info on all
the Beast Quest books, including the next exciting
series which features six brand-new Beasts!

Get 30% off all Beast Quest Books at www.beastquest.co.
Enter the code BEAST at the checkout.

All books priced at £4.99.
Special bumper editions priced at £5.99.

Orchard Books are available from all good bookshops, or can be ordered from our website: www.orchardbooks.co.uk, or telephone 01235 827702, or fax 01235 8227703.

FREE COLLECTOR CARDS INSIDE!

⟫⟫ Series 12: THE DARKEST HOUR ⟪⟪
COLLECT THEM ALL!

Three lands are in terrible danger from six new
Beasts. Tom must ride to the rescue!

SOLAK
SCOURGE OF THE SEA

978 1 40832 396 0

KAJIN
THE BEAST CATCHER

978 1 40832 397 7

ISSRILLA
THE CREEPING MENACE

978 1 40832 398 4

VIGRASH
THE CLAWED EAGLE

978 1 40832 399 1

MIRKA
THE ICE HORSE

978 1 40832 400 4

KAMA
THE FACELESS BEAST

978 1 40832 401 1

Series 13: THE WARRIOR'S ROAD
Out soon!

Meet six terrifying new Beasts!

Skuric the Forest Demon
Targro the Arctic Menace
Slivka the Cold-hearted Curse
Linka the Sky Conqueror
Vermok the Spiteful Scavenger
Koba the Ghoul of the Shadows

**Watch out for the next
Special Bumper
Edition
OUT June 2013!**

OUT NOVEMBER 2012!

MEET A NEW HERO OF AVANTIA

ISBN: 978 1 40831 868 3

Dark magic has been unleashed!

Evil boy-Wizard Maximus is using the stolen golden gauntlet to wreak havoc on Avantia. A new hero must stand up to him, and battle the Beasts!

Join Tom on his Beast Quests
and take part in a terrifying adventure
where YOU call the shots!

The Chronicles of Avantia

FROM THE DARK, A HERO ARISES...

Dare to enter the kingdom of Avantia.

A new evil arises in Avantia. Lord Derthsin has ordered his armies into the four corners of Avantia. If the four Beasts of Avantia can find their Chosen Riders they might have the strength to challenge Derthsin. But if they fail, the land of Avantia will be lost forever...

FIRST HERO, CHASING EVIL, CALL TO WAR, FIRE AND FURY- OUT NOW!

www.chroniclesofavantia.com

Read on for an exclusive extract of
CEPHALOX THE CYBERSQUID!

THE MERRYN TOUCH

The water was up to Max's knees and still rising. Soon it would reach his waist. Then his chest. Then his face.

I'm going to die down here, he thought.

He hammered on the dome with all his strength, but the plexiglass held firm.

Then he saw something pale looming through the dark water outside the submersible. A long, silvery spike. It must be the squid-creature, with one of its weird robotic attachments. Any second now it would smash the glass and finish him off...

There was a crash. The sub rocked. The silver spike thrust through the broken plexiglass. More water surged in. Then the spike withdrew and the water poured in faster. Max forced his way against the torrent to the opening. If he could just squeeze through the gap...

The jet of water pushed him back. He took one last deep breath, and then the water was over his head.

He clamped his mouth shut, struggling forwards, feeling the pressure on his lungs build.

Something gripped his arms, but it wasn't the squid's tentacle – it was a pair of hands, pulling him through the hole. The broken plexiglass scraped his sides and then he was through.

The monster was nowhere to be seen. In the dim underwater light, he made out the face of his rescuer. It was the Merryn girl, and next to her was a large silver swordfish.

She smiled at him.

Max couldn't smile back. He'd been saved from a metal coffin, only to swap it for a watery one. The pressure of the ocean squeezed him on every side. His lungs felt as though they were bursting.

He thrashed his limbs, rising upwards. He looked to where he thought the surface was, but saw nothing, only endless water. His cheeks puffed with the effort to hold in air. He let some of it out slowly, but it only made him want to breathe in more.

He knew he had no chance. He was too deep, he'd never make it to the surface in time. Soon he'd no longer be able to hold his breath. The water would swirl into his lungs and he'd die here, at the bottom of the sea. *Just like my mother*, he thought.

The Merryn girl rose up beside him, reached out and put her hands on his neck. Warmth seemed to flow from her fingers. Then the warmth turned to pain. What was happening? It got worse and worse, until Max felt as if his throat was being ripped open. Was she trying to kill him?

———

He struggled in panic, trying to push her off. His mouth opened and water rushed in.

That was it. He was going to die.

Then he realised something – the water was cool and sweet. He sucked it down into his lungs. Nothing had ever tasted so good.

He was breathing underwater!

He put his hands to his neck and found two soft, gill-like openings where the Merryn girl had touched him. His eyes widened in astonishment.

The girl smiled.

Other strange things were happening. Max found he could see more clearly. The water seemed lighter and thinner. He made out the shapes of underwater plants, rock formations and shoals of fish in the distance, which had been invisible before. And he didn't feel as if the ocean was crushing him any more.

Is this what it's like to be a Merryn? he wondered.

"I'm Lia," said the girl. "And this is Spike." She patted the swordfish on the back and it nuzzled against her.

"Hi, I'm Max." He clapped his hand to his mouth in shock. He was speaking the same strange language of sighs and whistles he'd heard the girl use when he first met her – but now it made sense, as if he was born to speak it.

"What have you done to me?" he said.

"Saved your life," said Lia. "You're welcome, by the way."

"Oh – don't think I'm not grateful – I am. But – you've turned me into a Merryn?"

The girl laughed. "Not exactly, but I've given you some Merryn powers. You can breathe underwater, speak our language, and your senses are much stronger. Come on – we need to get away from here. The Cyber Squid may come back."

In one graceful movement she slipped onto Spike's back. Max clambered on behind her.

"Hold tight," Lia said. "Spike – let's go!"

Max put his arms around the Merryn's waist. He was jerked backwards as the swordfish shot off through the water, but he managed to hold on.

They raced above underwater forests of gently waving fronds, and hills and valleys of rock. Max saw giant crabs scuttling over the seabed. Undersea creatures loomed up – jellyfish, an octopus, a school of dolphins – but Spike nimbly swerved round them.

"Where are we going?" Max asked.

"You'll see," Lia said over her shoulder.

"I need to find my dad," Max said. The crazy things that had happened in the last few moments had driven his father from his mind. Now it all came flooding back. Was his dad gone for good? "We have to do something! That monster's got my dad – and my dogbot too!"

"It's not the Cyber Squid who wants your father. It's the Professor who's *controlling* the Cyber Squid. I tried to warn you back at the city – but you wouldn't listen."

"I didn't understand you then!"

"You Breathers don't try to understand – that's your whole problem!"

"I'm trying now. What is that monster? And who is the Professor?"

"I'll explain everything when we arrive."

"Arrive where?"

The seabed suddenly fell away. A steep valley sloped down, leading way, way deeper than the ocean ridge Aquora was built on. The swordfish dived. The water grew darker.

Far below, Max saw a faint yellow glimmer. As he watched it grew bigger and brighter, until it became a vast undersea city of golden-glinting rock rushing up towards them. There were towers, spires, domes, bridges, courtyards, squares, gardens. A city as big as Aquora, and far more beautiful, at the bottom of the sea.

———

Max gasped in amazement. The water was
dark, but the city emitted a glow of its own
– a warm phosphorescent light that spilled
from the many windows. The rock sparkled.

———

Orange, pink and scarlet corals and seashells decorated the walls in intricate patterns.

"This is – amazing!" he said.

Lia turned round and smiled at him. "It's my home," she said. "Sumara!"

SEA QUEST

Calling all Adam Blade fans!

Are [...] avourite
autho [...] ea Ques

[...] ns

Simp [...] e form

?

re

?